The little caterpillar
who didn't want to become
a butterfly

Written by Judith Steinbacher

Illustrated by Antonia Nork

Translated by Reinhard Lindner

Zerwas Press

Tiny little eggs lay hidden deep in the dark green on velvety nettle leaves. Suddenly something moved, a little caterpillar hatched from one of the eggs. In addition to Carla, her brother Conrad and sister Cora also arrived. Soon many more caterpillars crawled around. Caterpillars are always very hungry, so they ate up all their own eggshells straight away. Only Carla looked around curiously. "What a waste of time," she said to Conrad and Cora, "come on, let's go and explore the world.

Carla, Conrad and Cora set off. They crept over leaves and stems. They met snails and beetles. Everything was new and tremendously exciting. "I'm hungry," Conrad said after a while and took a bite in the next leaf. Soon Cora had also had enough of the expedition. "Caterpillars have to eat," she said and stayed behind munching.

When Carla met her siblings that evening, she was tired but extremely happy. No other caterpillar had encountered so much. Most of the others hadn't left the nettles. They had eaten just the nearby leaves. They curled up full and lazy, and started to snore.

Carla stayed another day and night in her tree hollow.
Then she unfolded her wings and flew over fields and meadows.
She danced in the warm morning sun and sailed with the evening
wind. Her tender wings dazzled and sparkled in the sunlight.
Carla was over the moon. She couldn't understand anymore why
she hadn't wanted to become a butterfly. This summer Carla
would lay many eggs and would hide them under nettle leaves.
Many little caterpillars would hatch. They would eat and eat.
They would build cocoons and out would come exceptionally
beautiful butterflies.

But maybe once again one inquisitive little caterpillar wouldn't
want to become a butterfly...

After long dark winter days, the warm spring sun awoke
flowers and beetles. The cocoon in the hollow of the big,
old tree started to move. The cocoon burst and a little
body appeared. Then the fragile wings unfolded slowly
and dried in the warm air. Two eyes blinked curiously
in the sunlight. What a change! Carla, the little caterpillar,
was now an exceptionally beautiful butterfly.

The delightful sunny days were fading and a cold autumn wind was blowing the leaves from the trees. Animals and plants got ready for winter. The cocoon in the hollow of the big, old tree changed. It turned brown.

The first snowflakes fell gently down.

Late in summer the cocoons split and out
popped butterflies of breathtaking beauty.
Cora, Conrad and all the other butterflies
flew merrily and colourfully in the blue sky.

But what was Carla doing?

She still hung in her rigid cocoon
in the tree hollow.

"I want to be like that," whispered Carla and looked enthusiastically after the sparkling butterfly. Now she knew exactly what she wanted. She knew from her many excursions where the best and most delicious leaves would grow. She crawled as quickly as possible. When she arrived at these places, she immediately started to eat, and to eat, and to eat...
Soon her skin was too tight and cracked, making way for a bigger skin. Then she got the next skin and, then another. Soon she was a big, strong caterpillar. She found a secure and warm place in a hollow of a big, old tree. There she built a cocoon.

Suddenly the sky darkened and a huge and beautiful butterfly landed next to Carla. He majestically opened his wings. They sparkled and glittered in the sunshine. Carla opened her mouth wide; she had never seen anything so beautiful. "Why are you such a meagre little caterpillar?" asked the butterfly astonished, as he saw Carla. "If you don't hurry up and build a cocoon before the winter arrives, you will never become a butterfly. You must eat heartily!" "Then will I be like you?" asked Carla shyly. "Perhaps," answered the proud butterfly. He opened his wings and flew away smiling...

In the meantime, all the other caterpillars reached their
full growth. The big Cora built a cocoon first. She attached
a silky thread to a tree knot and now hung from it hard
and rigid. Conrad and all the others were ready, too.
Many green cocoons hung in the scrub and were waiting
to change into butterflies. Carla was left alone.
She played many different games but alone
it was no fun.

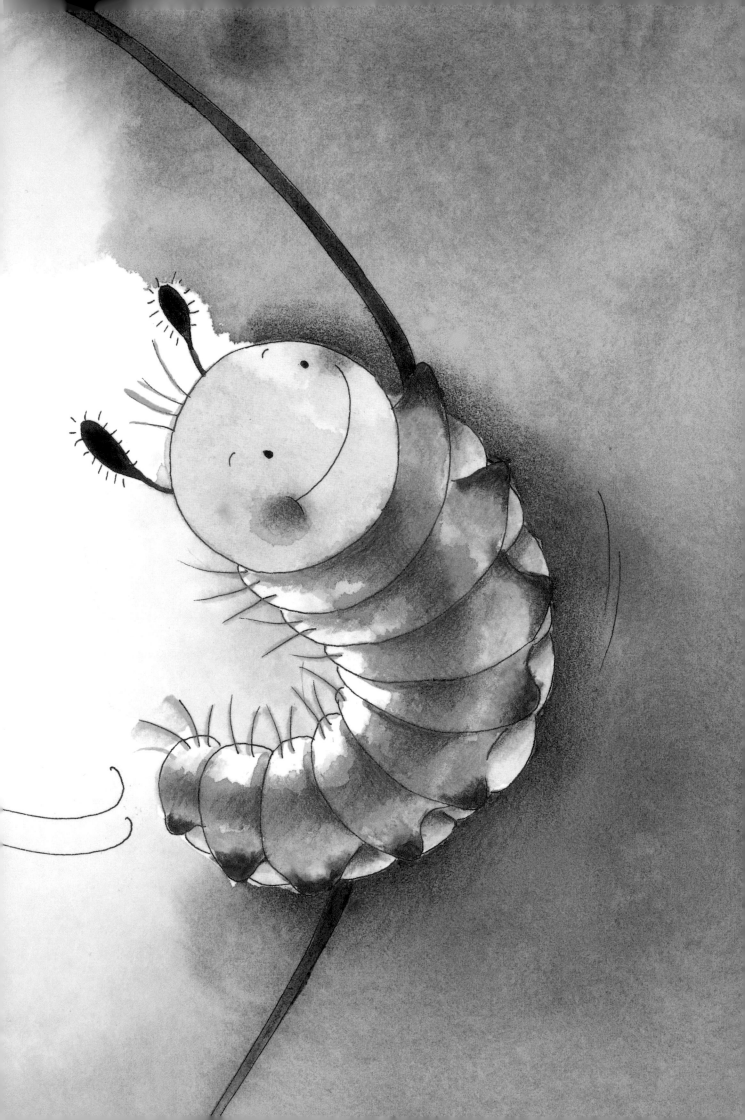

"I don't want to become a butterfly! Butterflies are stupid!
Come on Conrad! We can swing with the leaves, butterflies
can't!" pronounced Carla defiantly. She swung fiercely to
and fro. However, when Conrad tried to swing as well, he
slipped down and landed unpleasantly on the ground. "You ate
too much," Carla laughed at him. Conrad crawled laboriously
up the stem. "I will build a cocoon instead," he replied,
disgruntled. "Then you can swing alone." "What do you mean,
you will build a cocoon?" Carla asked incredulously. But
Conrad didn't answer.

"You all are sooo boring!" cried little Carla angrily.
She curled herself into a bobble and rolled down the next leaf
like a ball. "Let's play something funny together!" "Don't be
silly," responded Cora, "if you want to become a
butterfly, you haven't any time to play. You have to eat,
eat, eat...!" Carla's siblings were already double her size. Some
caterpillars had already cast off their first skin.

The next morning
sunrays shone through
the nettles and tickled Carla
on her nose. She was instantly
wide-awake. Dewdrops glittered and
sparkled around her. Carla crawled back
and forth between the dewdrops. She rolled
them in front of her and made them burst.
Then she discovered her mirror image in them.
That was particularly funny. "Oh no, wet,
water!" snorted Cora, as a big drop woke her
up with a start. She waggled herself
reluctantly and began to eat. Carla was
speechless. How could she think about
food, when so many exciting and
new things were around? The
other caterpillars also woke
up, stretched...and promptly
started to eat again.

Zerwas Press
4 Stourwood Mansions
Stourwood Avenue
Bournemouth
BH6 3PP

First published in the UK in 2002

Title of the original German edition:
Die kleine Raupe, die kein Schmetterling werden wollte
© 2001 Pattloch Verlag GmbH & Co. KG

English text © 2002 Reinhard Lindner

ISBN 0 9531830 1 7

A CIP catalogue record for this book is available from
The British Library

Printed & bound by SPC Print & Design Group, UK